D1123233

One fish
two fish
red fish
blue fish

一條魚
兩條魚
紅的魚
藍的魚

WITHDRAWN

By Dr. Seuss

文‧圖　蘇斯博士
譯　郝廣才

一條魚 兩條魚 紅的魚 藍的魚　　　　　　　　　　　　　斯博士小孩學讀書全集2

發行／1992 年 12 月 25 日初版 1 刷　　2002 年 7 月 5 日初版 5 刷

著／蘇斯博士

譯／郝廣才

責任編輯／郝廣才　張玲玲　劉思源

美術編輯／李純真　郭倖惠　陳素芳

發行人／王榮文　　出版發行／遠流出版事業股份有限公司　　　台北市汀州路3段184號7樓之5

行政院新聞局局版臺業字第1295號　　郵撥／0189456-1　　電話／(02)2365-3707　　傳真／(02)2365-7979

著作權顧問／蕭雄淋律師　　法律顧問／王秀哲律師・董安丹律師

印製／鴻柏印刷事業股份有限公司

YLib 遠流博識網 http://www.ylib.com　E-mail:ylib@yuanliou.ylib.com.tw

ISBN 957-32-1124-6　　　　　　　　　　　　　　　　　　　　　　　　NT$185

From there to here,
from here to there,
funny things
are everywhere.

從那裡到這裡，
從這裡到那裡，
不管在哪裡，
處處都有趣。

One fish

一^ㄧˋ條^ㄊㄧㄠˊ魚^ㄩˊ

two fish

兩^ㄌㄧㄤˇ條^ㄊㄧㄠˊ魚^ㄩˊ

red fish

紅^ㄏㄨㄥˊ的^ㄉㄜ魚^ㄩˊ

blue fish.

藍^ㄌㄢˊ的^ㄉㄜ魚^ㄩˊ

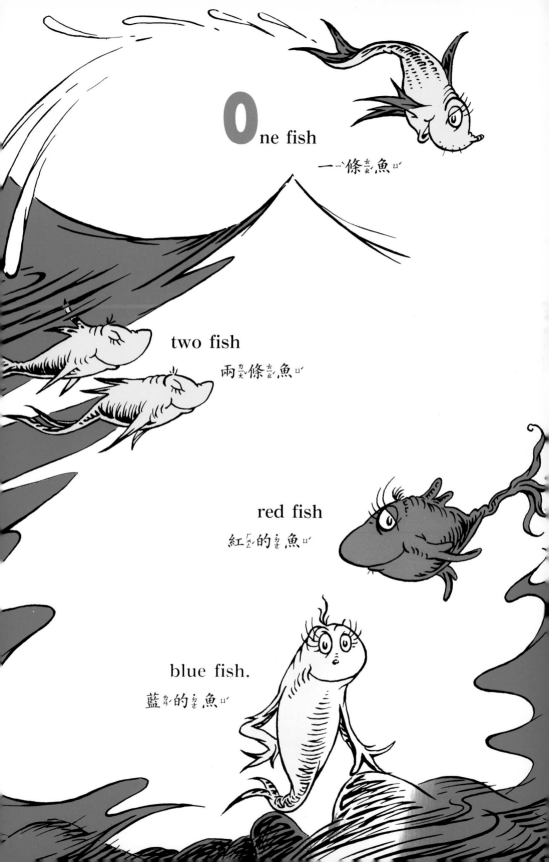

Black fish

黑(ㄏㄟ)的(ㄉㄜ)魚(ㄩ)

blue fish

藍(ㄌㄢ)的(ㄉㄜ)魚(ㄩ)

old fish

老(ㄌㄠ)的(ㄉㄜ)魚(ㄩ)

new fish.

小(ㄒㄧㄠ)的(ㄉㄜ)魚(ㄩ)

This one has
a little star.

這_{ㄓㄜˋ}條_{ㄊㄧㄠˊ}魚_{ㄩˊ}有_{ㄧㄡˇ}個_{ㄍㄜˋ}
小_{ㄒㄧㄠˇ}星_{ㄒㄧㄥ}星_{ㄒㄧㄥ}，

This one has a little car.
Say！ what a lot
of fish there are.

這_{ㄓㄜˋ}條_{ㄊㄧㄠˊ}魚_{ㄩˊ}開_{ㄎㄞ}車_{ㄔㄜ}滿_{ㄇㄢˇ}街_{ㄐㄧㄝ}跑_{ㄆㄠˇ}。
哇_{ㄨㄚ}！ 這_{ㄓㄜˋ}裡_{ㄌㄧˇ}的_{ㄉㄜ}魚_{ㄩˊ}兒_ㄦ真_{ㄓㄣ}不_{ㄅㄨˋ}少_{ㄕㄠˇ}。

Yes. Some are red. And some are blue.
Some are old. And some are new.

是ㄕˋ的ㄉㄜ˙，　有ㄧㄡˇ些ㄒㄧㄝ是ㄕˋ紅ㄏㄨㄥˊ的ㄉㄜ˙，　有ㄧㄡˇ些ㄒㄧㄝ是ㄕˋ藍ㄌㄢˊ的ㄉㄜ˙，
有ㄧㄡˇ些ㄒㄧㄝ是ㄕˋ老ㄌㄠˇ的ㄉㄜ˙，　有ㄧㄡˇ些ㄒㄧㄝ是ㄕˋ小ㄒㄧㄠˇ的ㄉㄜ˙。

Some are sad.

有ㄧㄡˇ些ㄒㄧㄝ魚ㄩˊ傷ㄕㄤ心ㄒㄧㄣ，

And some are glad.

有ㄧㄡˇ些ㄒㄧㄝ魚ㄩˊ開ㄎㄞ心ㄒㄧㄣ，

And some are very, very bad.

有_{ㄧㄡˇ}些_{ㄒㄧㄝ}魚_{ㄩˊ}壞_{ㄏㄨㄞˋ}心_{ㄒㄧㄣ}。

**Why are they
sad and glad and bad?
I do not know.
Go ask your dad.**

為_{ㄨㄟˋ}什_{ㄕㄣˊ}麼_{ㄇㄜ˙}魚_{ㄩˊ}會_{ㄏㄨㄟˋ}傷_{ㄕㄤ}心_{ㄒㄧㄣ}、
開_{ㄎㄞ}心_{ㄒㄧㄣ}和_{ㄏㄜˊ}壞_{ㄏㄨㄞˋ}心_{ㄒㄧㄣ}？
我_{ㄨㄛˇ}不_{ㄅㄨˋ}了_{ㄌㄧㄠˇ}解_{ㄐㄧㄝˇ}他_{ㄊㄚ}們_{ㄇㄣ˙}的_{ㄉㄜ˙}心_{ㄒㄧㄣ}，
去_{ㄑㄩˋ}找_{ㄓㄠˇ}爸_{ㄅㄚˋ}爸_{ㄅㄚ˙}問_{ㄨㄣˋ}一_ㄧ問_{ㄨㄣˋ}。

Some are thin.
有ㄧㄡˇ的ㄉㄜ˙是ㄕˋ瘦ㄕㄡˋ子ㄗ˙，

And some are fat.
The fat one has
a yellow hat.
有ㄧㄡˇ的ㄉㄜ˙是ㄕˋ胖ㄆㄤˋ子ㄗ˙，
胖ㄆㄤˋ子ㄗ˙頭ㄊㄡˊ上ㄕㄤˋ戴ㄉㄞˋ著ㄓㄜ˙
黃ㄏㄨㄤˊ帽ㄇㄠˋ子ㄗ˙。

From there to here,
from here to there,
funny things
are everywhere.

那裡到這裡，
這裡到那裡，
不管在哪裡，
處處都有趣。

Here are some
who like to run.
They run for fun
in the hot, hot sun.

有ㄧㄡˇ的ㄉㄜ˙喜ㄒㄧˇ歡ㄏㄨㄢ跑ㄆㄠˇ，
為ㄨㄟˋ了ㄌㄜ˙玩ㄨㄢˊ耍ㄕㄨㄚˇ
不ㄅㄨˋ怕ㄆㄚˋ太ㄊㄞˋ陽ㄧㄤˊ烤ㄎㄠˇ。

Oh me ! Oh my !
Oh me ! Oh my !
What a lot
of funny things go by.

哇ㄨㄚ哈ㄏㄚ！ 哇ㄨㄚ噻ㄙㄞ！
哇ㄨㄚ哈ㄏㄚ！ 哇ㄨㄚ噻ㄙㄞ！
這ㄓㄜ麼ㄇㄜ多ㄉㄨㄛ滑ㄏㄨㄚ稽ㄐㄧ古ㄍㄨ怪ㄍㄨㄞ
通ㄊㄨㄥ通ㄊㄨㄥ跑ㄆㄠ出ㄔㄨ來ㄌㄞ。

Some have two feet
and some have four.
Some have six feet
and some have more.

有ㄧ的ㄉㄜ兩ㄌㄧㄤ隻ㄓ腳ㄐㄧㄠ，
有ㄧ的ㄉㄜ四ㄙ隻ㄓ腳ㄐㄧㄠ，
有ㄧ的ㄉㄜ還ㄏㄞ有ㄧ六ㄌㄧㄡ隻ㄓ腳ㄐㄧㄠ，
比ㄅㄧ六ㄌㄧㄡ多ㄉㄨㄛ的ㄉㄜ也ㄧㄝ找ㄓㄠ得ㄉㄜ到ㄉㄠ。

Where do they come from?
I can't say.
But I bet they have come
a long, long way.

他們從哪裡來？
我說不明白。
但我打賭
是從遙遠的地方來。

We see them come.
We see them go.

看他們一一會兒過來，
一一會兒過去。

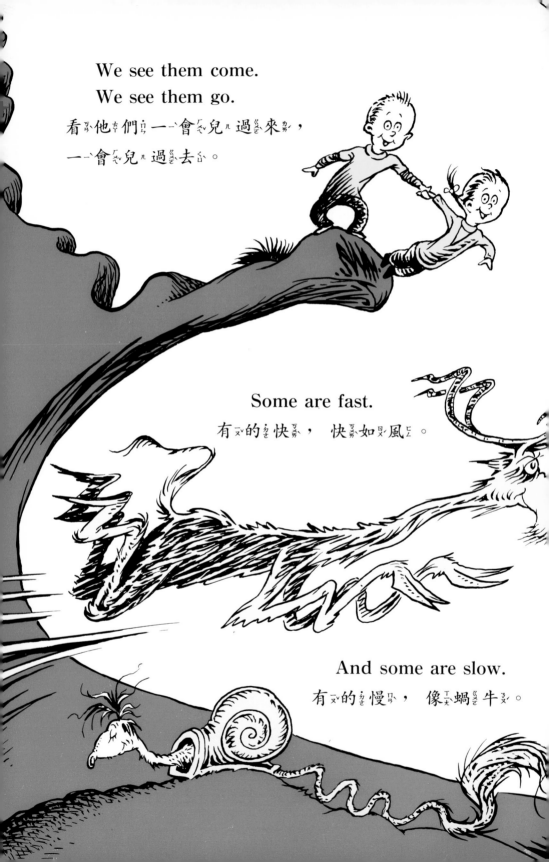

Some are fast.

有的快，　快如風。

And some are slow.

有的慢，　像蝸牛。

Some are high.

有_{ㄧㄡˇ}的_{ㄉㄜ˙}高_{ㄍㄠ}，　上_{ㄕㄤˋ}天_{ㄊㄧㄢ}空_{ㄎㄨㄥ}。

And some are low.

有_{ㄧㄡˇ}的_{ㄉㄜ˙}低_{ㄉㄧ}，　打_{ㄉㄚˇ}地_{ㄉㄧˋ}洞_{ㄉㄨㄥˋ}。

Not one of them
is like another.
Don't ask us why.
Go ask your mother.

他_{ㄊㄚ}們_{ㄇㄣ˙}沒_{ㄇㄟˊ}有_{ㄧㄡˇ}一_ㄧ個_{ㄍㄜˋ}長_{ㄓㄤˇ}得_{ㄉㄜ˙}像_{ㄒㄧㄤˋ}，

別_{ㄅㄧㄝˊ}問_{ㄨㄣˋ}我_{ㄨㄛˇ}們_{ㄇㄣ˙}為_{ㄨㄟˋ}什_{ㄕㄣˊ}麼_{ㄇㄜ˙}不_{ㄅㄨˋ}一_ㄧ樣_{ㄧㄤˋ}，

去_{ㄑㄩˋ}問_{ㄨㄣˋ}你_{ㄋㄧˇ}媽_{ㄇㄚ}怎_{ㄗㄣˇ}麼_{ㄇㄜ˙}會_{ㄏㄨㄟˋ}這_{ㄓㄜˋ}樣_{ㄧㄤˋ}？

Say !
Look at his fingers !
One, two, three……
How many fingers
do I see?

幾根手指看一看，
一二三來算一算。

One, two, three, four,
five, six, seven,
eight, nine, ten.
He has eleven !

一二三四五六七，
八、九、十、十一。
居然是十一！

Eleven !
This is something new.
I wish I had
eleven, too !

十一！
這事兒真新奇。
希望我的手指也是十加一！

Bump !
Bump !
Bump !
Did you ever ride a Wump?
We have a Wump
with just one hump.

哆ㄅㄨㄛ！
哆ㄅㄨㄛ！
哆ㄅㄨㄛ！
你ㄋㄧ有ㄧㄡ沒ㄇㄟ有ㄧㄡ騎ㄑㄧ過ㄍㄨㄛ駱ㄌㄨㄛ駝ㄊㄨㄛ？
我ㄨㄛ們ㄇㄣ有ㄧㄡ一ㄧ隻ㄓ一ㄧ個ㄍㄜ駝ㄊㄨㄛ峰ㄈㄥ
的ㄉㄜ駱ㄌㄨㄛ駝ㄊㄨㄛ。

But
we know a man
called Mr. Gump.
Mr. Gump has a seven hump Wump.
So......
if you like to go Bump！ Bump！
just jump on the hump of the Wump of Gump.

但我們認得一個人叫古伯。

古伯有一隻七個駝峰的駱駝。

如果你喜歡哆！ 哆！ 哆！

就快跳上古伯的駱駝。

Who am I?
My name is Ned.
I do not like
my little bed.

猜_{ㄘㄞ}猜_{ㄘㄞ}我_{ㄨㄛˇ}是_{ㄕˋ}誰_{ㄕㄟˊ}？
我_{ㄨㄛˇ}叫_{ㄐㄧㄠˋ}何_{ㄏㄜˊ}不_{ㄅㄨˋ}飛_{ㄈㄟ}。
我_{ㄨㄛˇ}的_{ㄉㄜ˙}床_{ㄔㄨㄤˊ}太_{ㄊㄞˋ}小_{ㄒㄧㄠˇ}，
實_{ㄕˊ}在_{ㄗㄞˋ}很_{ㄏㄣˇ}煩_{ㄈㄢˊ}惱_{ㄋㄠˇ}。

This is no good.
This is not right.
My feet stick out
of bed all night.

這_{ㄓㄜˋ}不_{ㄅㄨˋ}好_{ㄏㄠˇ}，　這_{ㄓㄜˋ}不_{ㄅㄨˋ}對_{ㄉㄨㄟˋ}，
腳_{ㄐㄧㄠˇ}一_ㄧ伸_{ㄕㄣ}，　出_{ㄔㄨ}床_{ㄔㄨㄤˊ}尾_{ㄨㄟˇ}，
整_{ㄓㄥˇ}個_{ㄍㄜˋ}晚_{ㄨㄢˇ}上_{ㄕㄤˋ}很_{ㄏㄣˇ}難_{ㄋㄢˊ}睡_{ㄕㄨㄟˋ}。

And when I pull them in,
Oh, dear !
My head sticks out of bed
up here !

當ㄉㄤ我ㄨㄛˇ把ㄅㄚˇ腳ㄐㄧㄠˇ塞ㄙㄞ進ㄐㄧㄣˋ床ㄔㄨㄤˊ裡ㄌㄧˇ邊ㄅㄧㄢ，
哎ㄞ喲ㄧㄡ，我ㄨㄛˇ的ㄉㄜ˙天ㄊㄧㄢ！
我ㄨㄛˇ的ㄉㄜ˙頭ㄊㄡˊ跑ㄆㄠˇ到ㄉㄠˋ床ㄔㄨㄤˊ頭ㄊㄡˊ外ㄨㄞˋ面ㄇㄧㄢˋ。

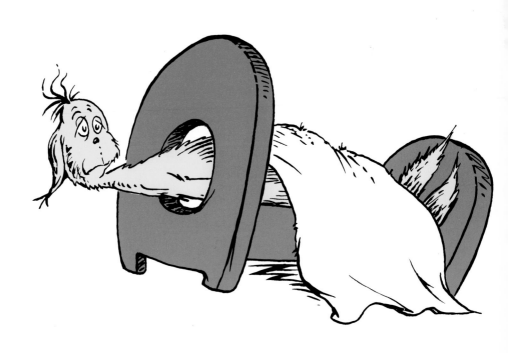

We like our bike.
It is made for three.
Our Mike
sits up in back,
you see.

我們喜歡我們的腳踏車。
它的座位有三個，
你看，我們的大麥克
坐在後頭呢！

We like our Mike
and this is why:
Mike does all the work
when the hills get high.

我ㄨˇ們ㄇㄣ˙喜ㄒㄧˇ歡ㄏㄨㄢ大ㄉㄚˋ麥ㄇㄞˋ克ㄎㄜˋ，
我ㄨˇ告ㄍㄠˋ訴ㄙㄨˋ你ㄋㄧˇ為ㄨㄟˋ什ㄕㄜˊ麼ㄇㄜ˙？
當ㄉㄤ車ㄔㄜ子ㄗ˙走ㄗㄡˇ到ㄉㄠˋ上ㄕㄤˋ坡ㄆㄛ，
一ㄧˋ切ㄑㄧㄝ都ㄉㄡ靠ㄎㄠˋ大ㄉㄚˋ麥ㄇㄞˋ克ㄎㄜˋ。

25

Hello there, Ned.
How do you do?
Tell me, tell me
what is new?
How are things
in your little bed?
What is new?
Please tell me, Ned.

喂ㄟ， 何ㄏㄜ不ㄅㄨ飛ㄈㄟ，
你ㄋㄧˇ好ㄏㄠˇ嗎ㄇㄚ？
告ㄍㄠˋ訴ㄙㄨˋ我ㄨㄛˇ， 告ㄍㄠˋ訴ㄙㄨˋ我ㄨㄛˇ
有ㄧㄡˇ什ㄕㄜˊ麼ㄇㄜ˙新ㄒㄧㄣ鮮ㄒㄧㄢ事ㄕˋ？
你ㄋㄧˇ的ㄉㄜ˙小ㄒㄧㄠˇ床ㄔㄨㄤˊ合ㄏㄜˊ不ㄅㄨ合ㄏㄜˊ適ㄕˋ
告ㄍㄠˋ訴ㄙㄨˋ我ㄨㄛˇ， 何ㄏㄜ不ㄅㄨ飛ㄈㄟ。

I do not like
this bed at all.
A lot of things
have come to call.
A cow, a dog, a cat, a mouse.
Oh！ what a bed！ Oh！ what a house！

我一點不喜歡我的床，
好多東西來嚷嚷。
有牛、 狗、 貓和老鼠，
哦！ 這張床太離譜。
哦！ 真是糟糕的房屋。

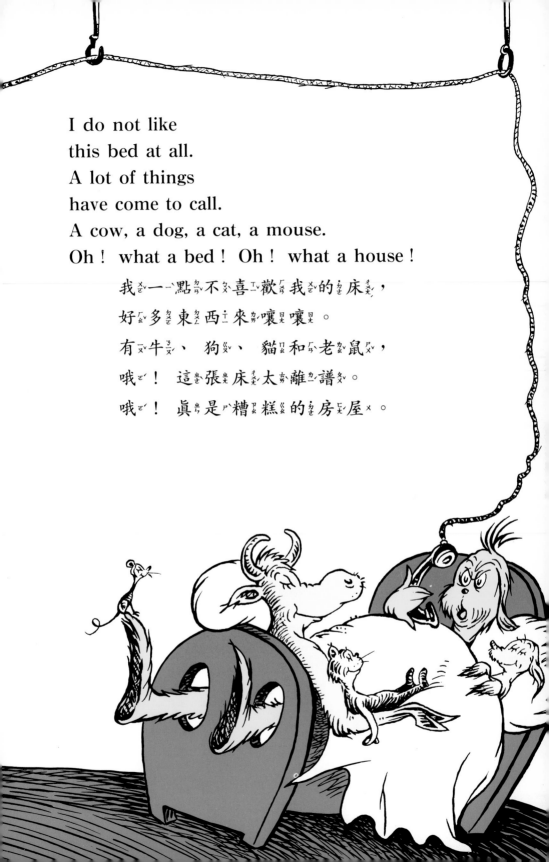

Oh, dear ! Oh, dear !
I can not hear.
Will you please
come over near?
Will you please look in my ear?
There must be something there, I fear.

哦，親愛的！我聽不見。
請你靠我近一點，
請看看我的耳朵，
我怕有什麼東西在裡面。

Say, look !
A bird was in your ear.
But he is out. So have no fear.
Again your ear can hear, my dear.

好，我看看！

有一隻鳥在你的耳朵裡面，

不過別害怕，牠已經在外邊，

親愛的，你又可以聽得見。

My hat is old.
My teeth are gold.
I have a bird
I like to hold.
My shoe is off.
My foot is cold.

我ㄨㄛˇ的ㄉㄜ˙帽ㄇㄠˋ子ㄗ˙是ㄕˋ舊ㄐㄧㄡˋ的ㄉㄜ˙，
我ㄨㄛˇ的ㄉㄜ˙牙ㄧㄚˊ齒ㄔˇ是ㄕˋ金ㄐㄧㄣ的ㄉㄜ˙。
我ㄨㄛˇ有ㄧㄡˇ一ㄧˋ隻ㄓ鳥ㄋㄧㄠˇ，
我ㄨㄛˇ喜ㄒㄧˇ歡ㄏㄨㄢ抱ㄅㄠˋ著ㄓㄜ˙。
我ㄨㄛˇ的ㄉㄜ˙鞋ㄒㄧㄝˊ子ㄗ˙掉ㄉㄧㄠˋ了ㄌㄜ˙，
我ㄨㄛˇ的ㄉㄜ˙腳ㄐㄧㄠˇ好ㄏㄠˇ冷ㄌㄥˇ。

My shoe is off.
My foot is cold.
I have a bird
I like to hold.
My hat is old.
My teeth are gold.
And now
my story
is all told.

我ㄨㄛˇ的ㄉㄜ˙鞋ㄒㄧㄝˊ子ㄗ˙掉ㄉㄧㄠˋ了ㄌㄜ˙，
我ㄨㄛˇ的ㄉㄜ˙腳ㄐㄧㄠˇ好ㄏㄠˇ冷ㄌㄥˇ。
我ㄨㄛˇ有ㄧㄡˇ一ㄧ隻ㄓ鳥ㄋㄧㄠˇ，
我ㄨㄛˇ喜ㄒㄧˇ歡ㄏㄨㄢ抱ㄅㄠˋ著ㄓㄜ˙。
我ㄨㄛˇ的ㄉㄜ˙帽ㄇㄠˋ子ㄗ˙是ㄕˋ舊ㄐㄧㄡˋ的ㄉㄜ˙，
我ㄨㄛˇ的ㄉㄜ˙牙ㄧㄚˊ齒ㄔˇ是ㄕˋ金ㄐㄧㄣ的ㄉㄜ˙。
現ㄒㄧㄢˋ在ㄗㄞˋ我ㄨㄛˇ的ㄉㄜ˙故ㄍㄨˋ事ㄕˋ說ㄕㄨㄛ完ㄨㄢˊ了ㄌㄜ˙。

We took a look.
We saw a Nook.
On his head
he had a hook.
On his hook
he had a book.
On his book.
was "How to Cook."

東看看，西瞧瞧，
儂克頭上戴帽子，
帽子上面有勾子，
勾子掛著一本書，
原來是一本食譜。

We saw him sit
and try to cook.
He took a look
at the book on
the hook.

How
to
Cook

But a Nook can't read,
so a Nook can't cook.
SO......
what good to a Nook
is a hook cook book?

儂ㄋㄨㄥ克ㄎㄜˋ坐ㄗㄨㄛˋ著ㄓㄜ˙想ㄒㄧㄤˇ要ㄧㄠˋ做ㄗㄨㄛˋ點ㄉㄧㄢˇ食ㄕˊ物ㄨˋ，
他ㄊㄚ看ㄎㄢˋ著ㄓㄜ˙勾ㄍㄡ子ㄗˇ上ㄕㄤˋ的ㄉㄜ˙書ㄕㄨ，
但ㄉㄢˋ他ㄊㄚ只ㄓˇ能ㄋㄥˊ看ㄎㄢˋ不ㄅㄨˊ會ㄏㄨㄟˋ讀ㄉㄨˊ，
所ㄙㄨㄛˇ以ㄧˇ他ㄊㄚ做ㄗㄨㄛˋ不ㄅㄨˋ出ㄔㄨ食ㄕˊ物ㄨˋ，
所ㄙㄨㄛˇ以ㄧˇ啦ㄌㄚ˙……
食ㄕˊ譜ㄆㄨˇ這ㄓㄜˋ本ㄅㄣˇ書ㄕㄨ對ㄉㄨㄟˋ他ㄊㄚ
有ㄧㄡˇ沒ㄇㄟˊ有ㄧㄡˇ好ㄏㄠˇ處ㄔㄨˋ？

The moon was out
and we saw some sheep.
We saw some sheep
take a walk in their sleep.

月光光光，　大白羊，
大白羊在夢鄉，
一邊睡覺一邊逛。

By the light of the moon,
by the light of a star,
they walked all night
from near to far.

天_{ㄊㄧㄢ}上_{ㄕㄤ}的_{ㄉㄜ}明_{ㄇㄧㄥ}月_{ㄩㄝ}光_{ㄍㄨㄤ}，
天_{ㄊㄧㄢ}上_{ㄕㄤ}的_{ㄉㄜ}星_{ㄒㄧㄥ}閃_{ㄕㄢ}亮_{ㄌㄧㄤ}，
大_{ㄉㄚ}白_{ㄅㄞ}羊_{ㄧㄤ}走_{ㄗㄡ}了_{ㄌㄜ}整_{ㄓㄥ}個_{ㄍㄜ}晚_{ㄨㄢ}上_{ㄕㄤ}，
走_{ㄗㄡ}到_{ㄉㄠ}很_{ㄏㄣ}遠_{ㄩㄢ}的_{ㄉㄜ}地_{ㄉㄧ}方_{ㄈㄤ}。

I would never walk.
I would take a car.

我_{ㄨㄛ}從_{ㄘㄨㄥ}來_{ㄌㄞ}走_{ㄗㄡ}路_{ㄌㄨ}不_{ㄅㄨ}用_{ㄩㄥ}腳_{ㄐㄧㄠ}，
我_{ㄨㄛ}開_{ㄎㄞ}著_{ㄓㄜ}車_{ㄔㄜ}子_ㄗ跑_{ㄆㄠ}。

I do not like
this one so well.
All he does
is yell, yell, yell.
I will not have this one about.
When he comes in
I put him out.

我不大喜歡這野獸，
他只會吼、 吼、 吼。
和他一起真難受，
他一進來我就要他到外頭。

This one is
quiet as a mouse.
I like to have him
in the house.

他像老鼠靜靜不開口，
我喜歡他在屋裡頭。

At our house
we open cans.
We have to open
many cans.
And that is why
we have a Zans.

A Zans for cans
is very good.
Have you a Zans for cans?
You should.

房子裡，　開罐頭，

再多罐頭也不愁，

因為我們有鑽牛。

鑽牛開罐頭，

眞是有一手。

你有沒有這樣的好朋友？

應該養一頭。

I like to box.
How I like to box !
So, every day,
I box a Gox.

我ㄨㄛˇ愛ㄞˋ打ㄉㄚˇ拳ㄑㄩㄢˊ擊ㄐㄧˊ，
我ㄨㄛˇ有ㄧㄡˇ高ㄍㄠ大ㄉㄚˋ力ㄌㄧˋ，
天ㄊㄧㄢ天ㄊㄧㄢ陪ㄆㄟˊ我ㄨㄛˇ打ㄉㄚˇ，
從ㄘㄨㄥˊ來ㄌㄞˊ不ㄅㄨˋ休ㄒㄧㄡ息ㄒㄧˊ。

In yellow socks
I box my Gox.
I box in yellow
Gox box socks.

我ㄨㄛˇ戴ㄉㄞˋ黃ㄏㄨㄤˊ色ㄙㄜˋ拳ㄑㄩㄢˊ擊ㄐㄧ套ㄊㄠˋ，

和ㄏㄜˊ高ㄍㄠ大ㄉㄚˋ力ㄌㄧˋ練ㄌㄧㄢˋ幾ㄐㄧˇ招ㄓㄠ，

黃ㄏㄨㄤˊ色ㄙㄜˋ黃ㄏㄨㄤˊ色ㄙㄜˋ拳ㄑㄩㄢˊ擊ㄐㄧ套ㄊㄠˋ，

高ㄍㄠ大ㄉㄚˋ力ㄌㄧˋ也ㄧㄝˇ有ㄧㄡˇ一ㄧ套ㄊㄠˋ。

It is fun to sing
if you sing with a Ying.
My Ying can sing
like anything.

I sing high
and my Ying sings low,
and we are not too bad,
you know.

和大聲哥一起唱歌。
真是快樂。
大聲哥唱歌
真是了不得。

我唱高音，
大聲哥唱低音。
我們唱得真不錯，
聽過的人都這樣說。

This one,
I think,
is called
a Yink.
He likes to wink,
he likes to drink.

這⽚個⾜寶⽊貝⽛
我⽊想⽟是⽑叫⽟美⽆胃⽊。
他⽅喜⽟歡⽉眨⾂眼⽆睛⽴，
他⽅喜⽟歡⽉喝⾜水⽊。

He likes to drink, and drink, and drink.
The thing he likes to drink
is ink.
The ink he likes to drink is pink.
He likes to wink and drink pink ink.
SO...
if you have a lot of ink,
then you should get
a Yink, I think.

喝水，　喝水，　喝水，
他喜歡喝墨水，
眨眼睛，　喝墨水，
他最喜歡喝粉紅色的墨水。
如果你的墨水有一大堆，
別浪費，　請你給美胃。

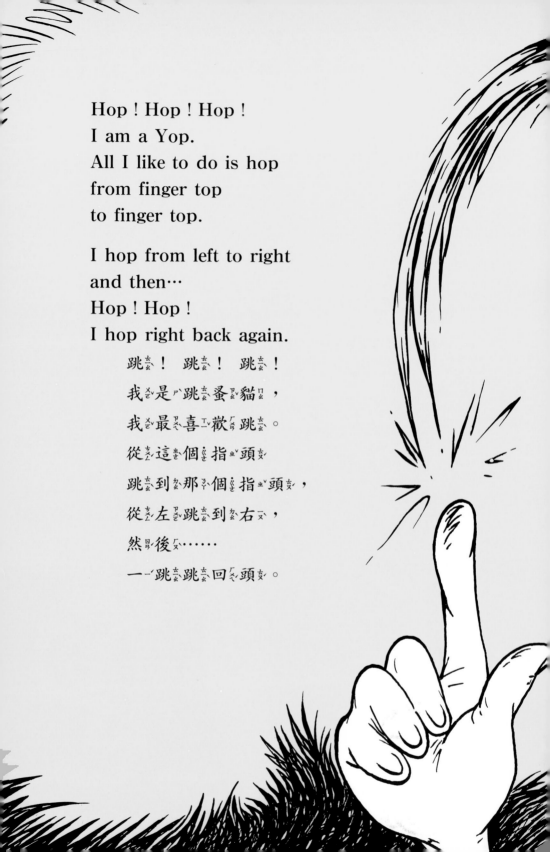

Hop ! Hop ! Hop !
I am a Yop.
All I like to do is hop
from finger top
to finger top.

I hop from left to right
and then…
Hop ! Hop !
I hop right back again.

跳！ 跳！ 跳！
我是跳蚤貓，
我最喜歡跳。
從這個指頭
跳到那個指頭，
從左跳到右，
然後……
一跳跳回頭。

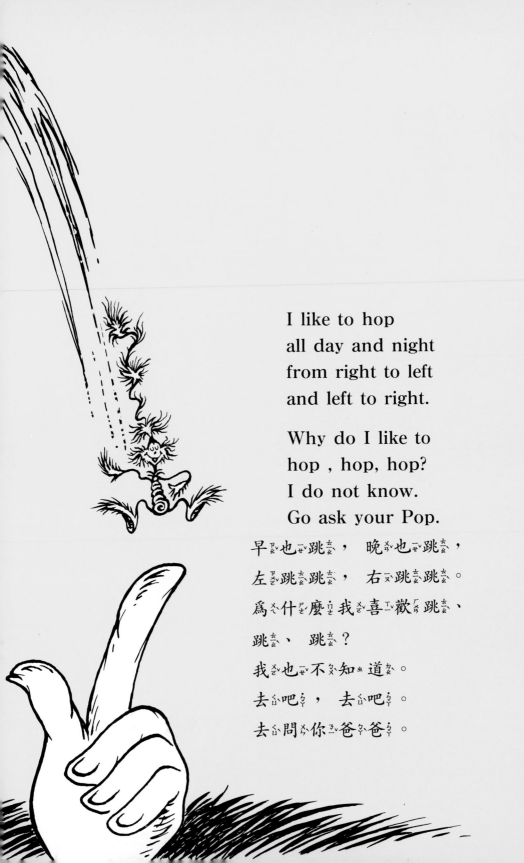

I like to hop
all day and night
from right to left
and left to right.

Why do I like to
hop , hop, hop?
I do not know.
Go ask your Pop.

早也跳，　晚也跳，
左跳跳，　右跳跳。
為什麼我喜歡跳、
跳、　跳？
我也不知道。
去吧，　去吧。
去問你爸爸。

Brush ! Brush !
Brush ! Brush !
Comb ! Comb !
Comb ! Comb !
Blue hair
is fun
to brush and comb.
All girls who like
to brush and comb
should have a pet
like this at home.

刷啊！ 刷啊！

刷啊！ 刷啊！

梳啊！ 梳啊！

梳啊！ 梳啊！

刷刷梳梳藍色的頭髮

真是好玩呀。

哪個女孩喜歡又梳又刷，

應該養這樣的寵物在家。

Who is this pet?
Say !
He is wet.

You never yet
met a pet,
I bet,
as wet as they let
this wet pet get.

這是誰？
看他全身是水。
我敢打賭你沒有看過，
這樣全身溼透的傢伙。

Did you ever
fly a kite
in bed?

你ㄋㄧˇ曾ㄘㄥˊ不ㄅㄨˋ曾ㄘㄥˊ
在ㄗㄞˋ床ㄔㄨㄤˊ上ㄕㄤˋ放ㄈㄤˋ風ㄈㄥ箏ㄓㄥ？

Did you ever walk
with ten cats
on your head?

你ㄋㄧˇ有ㄧㄡˇ沒ㄇㄟˊ有ㄧㄡˇ
一ㄧ邊ㄅㄧㄢ走ㄗㄡˇ路ㄌㄨˋ
一ㄧ邊ㄅㄧㄢ抱ㄅㄠˋ十ㄕˊ隻ㄓ貓ㄇㄠ
頂ㄉㄧㄥˇ在ㄗㄞˋ頭ㄊㄡˊ？

Did you ever milk
this kind of cow?
Well, we can do it.
We know how.

這種牛的奶你有沒有擠過？

我們知道怎麼做，

我們做得真不錯。

If you never did,
you should.
These things are fun
and fun is good.

如果你從沒這經驗，

你應該試試。

這些事情很好玩，

好玩是好事。

Hello !
Hello !
Are you there?
Hello !
I called you up
to say hello.
I said hello.
Can you hear me, Joe?

喂！喂！
你在不在家？
喂！我在叫你啊！
快說喂。
我說喂，
王二麻，你能聽見嗎？

Oh, no.
I can not hear your call.
I can not hear your call at all.
This is not good
and I know why.
A mouse has cut the wire.
Good－by!

哦，不行。

我聽不見你的說話聲，

我一點都聽不見你的說話聲。

這不是好事情，

我知道為什麼會發生，

有一隻老鼠剪斷電話線，

再見！

From near to far
from here to there,
funny things are everywhere.

從近到遠，
從這裡到那裡，
不管在哪裡，
處處都有趣。

These yellow pets
are called the Zeds.
They have one hair
up on their heads.
Their hair grows fast...
so fast, they say,
they need a hair cut
every day.

黃毛小寵物，
名字叫阿福。
頭上一根毛，
生長很快速。
天天剪頭髮，
頭也不會禿。

Who am I?
My name is Ish.
On my hand I have a dish.

猜猜我是誰？
我叫吃不肥。
我有大金盤，
永遠打不碎。

I have this dish
to help me wish.

我有大金盤，
幫我來許願。

When I wish to make a wish
I wave my hand with a big swish swish.
Then I say,"I wish for fish ! "
And I get fish right on my dish.

當ㄉㄤ我ㄨㄛˇ要ㄧㄠˋ許ㄒㄩˇ願ㄩㄢˋ，
搖ㄧㄠˊ搖ㄧㄠˊ手ㄕㄡˇ， 轉ㄓㄨㄢˇ三ㄙㄢ圈ㄑㄩㄢ，
魚ㄩˊ來ㄌㄞˊ也ㄧㄝˇ， 說ㄕㄨㄛ一ㄧˊ遍ㄆㄧㄢˋ，
魚ㄩˊ兒ㄦ魚ㄩˊ兒ㄦ就ㄐㄧㄡˋ出ㄔㄨ現ㄒㄧㄢˋ。

So...
if you wish to wish a wish,
you may swish for fish
with my Ish wish dish.

想ㄒㄧㄤˇ許ㄒㄩˇ願ㄩㄢˋ， 並ㄅㄧㄥˋ不ㄅㄨˋ難ㄋㄢˊ，
有ㄧㄡˇ了ㄌㄜ我ㄨㄛˇ的ㄉㄜ大ㄉㄚˋ金ㄐㄧㄣ盤ㄆㄢˊ，
實ㄕˊ現ㄒㄧㄢˋ願ㄩㄢˋ望ㄨㄤˋ很ㄏㄣˇ簡ㄐㄧㄢˇ單ㄉㄢ。

At our house
we play out back.
We play a game
called Ring the Gack.

大角鹿，　叫阿西，
我們從來也不騎。
在家一起玩遊戲，
丟圈圈，　套阿西。

Would you like to play this game?
Come down !
We have the only
Gack in town.

喜不喜歡這遊戲？
請你不要急，
全城只有我們有阿西，
總有一天輪到你。

Look what we found
in the park
in the dark.
We will take him home.
We will call him Clark.

天這麼黑，

公園這麼大，

我們找到娃娃牙，

要帶他回家。

He will live at our house.
He will grow and grow.
Will our mother like this?
We don't know.

娃娃牙， 住我家

他會一天天長大。

我們的媽媽

會不會喜歡他？

And now
good night.
It is time to sleep.
So we will sleep
with our pet Zeep.

讓我們說一聲晚安，
現在到了睡覺時間。
大寶貝， 淘大尾，
我們和他一起睡。

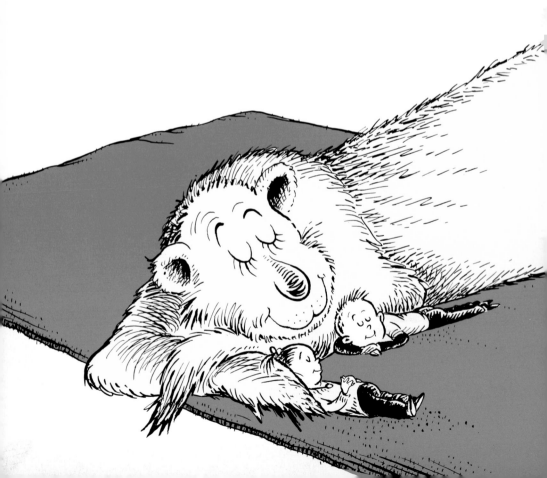

Today is gone. Today was fun.
Tomorrow is another one.
Every day,
from here to there,
funny things are everywhere.

今天已過去，
今天真有趣。
明天會再來，
天天都新奇。
這裡到那裡，
處處都有趣。